CALL OF CTHULHU'S HEART

A SHORT TENTACLE MONSTER ROMANCE

FAE RINGS
BOOK THREE

JAX WILDER

Published by Rainbow Quartz Publishing

RQPublishing.com

RainbowQuartzPublishing@gmail.com

Edmonds, WA 98026

ISBN: 978-1-961714-69-4

Cover design by Miranda Townsend

Edited by Miranda Townsend

First Edition: March 2025

For my tentacle loving readers.

CHAPTER ONE

Coral Cove has always felt a little bit like a dream, caught somewhere between the everyday and the fantastical. The kind of place where time seems to slow and the lines between reality and imagination blur. I feel it every time I wander down Main Street, the ocean breeze carrying more than just salt and sun. There's an undercurrent here, something that pulls at you, whispering of secrets hidden beneath the waves and magic woven into the cobblestones.

Locals have a saying about this town: you never buy what you came in for; you buy what came for you. Tourists repeat it like it's cute. The rest of us say it softer, like a prayer, or a warning.

I work at the Maritime Center, spending my

days teaching visitors about kelp forests and the patient strength of barnacles. I love the ocean's logic, the way a tide pool becomes a little kingdom if you know where to look. It's rewarding work. It's also very tidy. Safe. Last month, Sofia packed her tiny car and left for a research fellowship in Monterey. Liam got into grad school; Amber is sailing with a coral restoration team. I smiled and hugged them and meant every congratulations. Then I went home to my studio apartment and watched the light crawl across the wall until it was dark.

Sometimes I want something that refuses to be cataloged. Something I can't file under habitat or behavior. A touch of magic, maybe. A little trouble. And if there's one place in Coral Cove that feels like it might hold the key to that kind of escape, it's Lilly Drake.

The little chime above the door rings as I step inside, and immediately I'm wrapped in the shop's honeyed warmth. It smells of aged wood and lavender, with a hint of something else, something rich and mineral, like rain on hot stone. Sunlight filters through the stained glass windows, casting ribbons of color over cases and shelves. Everywhere I look, there are treasures: strands of sea glass that catch the light like water, charms shaped like moons and tiny ships, jars of sand labeled with places I've never been.

Rainbow Rivers stands behind the counter, her lavender hair falling in soft waves around her shoulders. The small, iridescent wings pinned at her back flutter when she laughs—a shop quirk, people say, but I've never seen the mechanism. She looks up as I enter, a knowing smile curving her lips.

"Ah, Maddison," she says, her voice a lilting melody. "Back again?"

I shrug, but I can't help the grin that tugs at my mouth. "What can I say? This place has a pull I can't explain."

"That's because Lilly Drake is a house of possibilities," Rainbow says. "It draws in the ones who are searching—whether they know what for or not."

I wander the aisles, letting my fingers drift over necklaces made of sea glass and charms shaped like tiny silver nautiluses. A thrum hums beneath it all, the way a shell holds the ocean's breath. I tell myself it's the building settling, the radiator ticking, anything ordinary. But the hum threads through my bones like a remembered lullaby.

That's when I see it—a flash of silver nestled among the other jewelry, a ring that catches the light in a way that feels deliberate. It's displayed off to the side, not hidden, but not the first thing you'd notice. The band is simple, the metal a soft, aged sheen. The stone at its center is not quite opal, not quite pearl, and as I angle it, it throws thin rainbows across the glass case. Along the band, tiny designs twist and curve: wave lines braided with something sharper, almost like teeth, and a small sigil I can't name—three spirals joined at their points, forming a kind of crown. The shapes are beautiful, but they make the skin on my arms lift as if from a cold draft.

I don't realize how long I stand there until Rainbow's voice pulls me back.

"It's calling to you, isn't it?" she asks quietly.

My throat is dry. "It feels... alive."

Rainbow comes around the counter with a key I've never seen her use. She unlocks the case and lifts the ring with careful fingers. Up close, it's warm, as if it's been resting in sunlight. Or as if it's been waiting.

"This isn't just a piece of jewelry, Maddison," she says. "It's a gateway. A connection to a world beyond ours—a world where desires and dangers walk side by side."

A prickling moves up my spine. I've heard stories about people in Coral Cove who wanted too much and got exactly that. A girl who walked into the fog at Pelican Point and swore the statues turned their heads to watch her pass. A fisherman who claimed the ocean spoke to him in the dead of winter and then sold his boat and never went near the water again.

"What kind of world?" I ask. The question comes out before I can stop it.

Rainbow studies me, her smile fading into something more serious. "One that offers what you most ache for—and collects what you didn't realize you'd wagered." She holds the ring just out of reach. "Most who wear it aren't ready."

"I am," I say, too fast.

Her brows rise. "Then tell me. What is it you want that you can't catalog or teach on a guided tour?"

The honest answer lands in my mouth before pride can interfere. "To feel like my life is moving again. Like I'm not watching from shore while everyone else sails away." I breathe out. "To be part of something that matters."

Rainbow nods once, like a bell struck softly. "And what will you leave behind at the door? Every door takes a toll. Even this one."

I think of the careful lists on my fridge, the

budget spreadsheet, the way I've learned to choose safe over sorry so many times it's become reflex. "Control," I whisper, surprising myself. "The kind that keeps me small."

Rainbow's expression flickers—approval, worry, something like regret. Then she tilts the ring so the light finds its heart. It thrums in her palm, almost a heartbeat.

"It's not the ring that chooses," she says. "It's what waits on the other side. If you put this on, you should know: doors open both ways, but some refuse to close."

Her words should send me backing away, thanking her politely, promising to think about it. Instead they root me where I am. The ache in my chest sharpens, not painful exactly, just precise. I hold out my hand.

"I'll take it."

For a moment, I think she'll refuse. Instead she slips the ring into a small velvet pouch and places it in my palm. Her fingers linger on mine, cool and steady.

"Be careful, Maddison," she murmurs. "This ring knows where it belongs. It might let you in, but it doesn't always let you go."

A breath shivers through me. "Is there anything

else I should know?"

Rainbow's gaze holds mine. "Listen for the rhythm that isn't yours. If you hear it, don't mistake it for a welcome."

I nod like I understand. Maybe I do. Maybe I don't. Either way, the decision sits in my pocket, heavier than the pouch suggests.

Outside, noon light glitters on the water, and the familiar sounds of Coral Cove surge around me—the crash of waves, the chatter of tourists, the squeal of a bike brake and someone laughing at nothing in particular. The normalcy is almost startling. I walk toward the boardwalk by instinct, toward the blue that has always been my compass. Seagulls wheel lazy arcs overhead. A dog barks down by the tide line. The world keeps being the world.

But the pouch presses against my thigh like a second pulse.

On the steps to the beach, I stop. I take the ring out, holding it up so the sun pours through the strange stone. That faint, impossible shimmer moves inside it, rainbows sliding like oil on water. The carvings catch the light—the braid of wave and tooth, the small crown of spirals. It is beautiful the way a riptide is beautiful from a distance.

I slide the ring onto my finger.

The world tightens around me, the way the air goes still before a storm. A slow, steady beat thrums at the edge of hearing, and for half a second I think it's my heart, but it's not. It's bigger. Wider. The ring's rhythm rises to meet it, and something inside me aligns with a click I feel in my teeth.

I close my eyes. The sound fills me. It isn't music. It isn't silence. It's the measure of something old.

When I open my eyes, Coral Cove is still here—boardwalk, beach, the bright umbrellas. But everything looks sharpened, edges inked darker. The blue in the bay is a blue I don't have a name for. For one breath, all the gulls midair hang like cutouts. The second shadow beneath my feet—one I swear wasn't there a moment ago—tilts toward the ocean as if it's standing on a different clock.

Down the beach, a little boy stops and stares, not at me but at my hand, his mouth parted like he recognizes something and can't place from where. His mother tugs him along, not noticing.

I breathe in. The air tastes faintly of copper and lilac. The ring warms, then cools, then settles like it has found its home.

Somewhere beneath the familiar tide, a deeper current moves, slow and vast, counting in a language my body is suddenly certain it once knew.

I look at the water and smile, even as a shiver tickles the back of my neck. Whatever awaits me, I know one thing for sure, my life is no longer standing still.

And in the glass of the shop window behind me, just for a heartbeat, my reflection turns its face toward the sea before I do.

CHAPTER TWO

At first, Coral Cove is still there—or at least the shape of it. The boardwalk stretches at my back, the gulls suspended in their impossible stillness, the ocean holding its breath. But as I blink, the edges of the town ripple like ink dropped in water, colors bleeding and reforming until the familiar is washed away.

When I open my eyes again, the veil has thinned past breaking. Coral Cove is not gone so much as rewritten, its bones dissolved into something stranger, something older.

The sky churns like a living tide, violet collapsing into turquoise, crimson splitting open gold. The colors hum against my teeth, alive, as if the heavens themselves are breathing. For a moment I think if I reached high enough, the sky would wrap around my hand like silk.

The sand beneath me has been replaced by a carpet of shimmering moss that glows faintly—pale blue shifting to lavender, then back again, undecided. Each step presses into it and the ground springs back as though it's breathing with me, watching, waiting. A pulse echoes beneath it, the same rhythm I felt in the ring, slow and impossibly vast.

The air thickens, sweet and rotting all at once: overripe fruit tangled with the scent of wet soil after a storm. It fills my lungs until I feel weighted, like my bones want to sink into this place and root themselves. My skin prickles, caught between welcome and warning.

That's when I hear it.

A whisper. Not quite a voice, not quite a sound. It threads through my body like vibration, humming in the hollow of my chest. For an instant, I'm floating, weightless, as though the world itself is holding me suspended in its song.

The moss ripples beneath me, guiding my steps forward. Around me, alien plants rear up, their translucent leaves webbed with veins of light that pulse in time with the world's rhythm. Tendrils brush my arms as I pass, trailing warmth into my skin as though claiming me. The whisper grows more insistent, not words but an invitation, tugging at the rawest parts of me.

I move beneath glowing arches of vine, past flowers too large and too bright to belong to earth. One curls around my fingers, petal warm as flesh, its scent dizzying, heady, nearly intoxicating. A shiver rolls down my spine, heat gathering low in my belly as the air hums with anticipation.

Through a haze of mist, something vast rises: a structure, or perhaps a growth, older than architecture. Its surface writhes with symbols that shift when I look too long, wet stone glowing with a faint inner heat. It feels less like a building and more like the earth itself has chosen to open its chest.

The whisper crescendos, pressing against my thoughts, urging surrender. My palm meets the slick wall, and the carvings flare under my touch, bright as burning coals. The stone pulses once, twice, in time with the hammer of my own heart—until I can no longer tell which rhythm belongs to me.

And then it stirs.

A presence vast and ancient coils around me, shadow-warm, terrifying and tender at once. My body arches, trembling, caught between terror and desire. The symbols blaze brighter, and I gasp as fire floods through me, filling every vein, every nerve, until I am nothing but heat and heartbeat.

Images burst behind my eyes: oceans swallowing stars, endless corridors of light, mouths opening in the dark. None of them stay long enough to understand, only long enough to remind me how small I am, how fragile. And yet the presence presses closer, as if I am not prey but something it has chosen.

The whisper returns, now laced with a strange intimacy. It doesn't speak in language, but I understand: *more, come closer, give.* My thoughts blur, scattered like leaves in a storm.

I lean into the stone, my fingers splayed across symbols that writhe beneath my touch. The heat climbs higher, pooling low in my belly until I'm shaking with it, torn between dread and the aching sweetness of surrender.

I don't know how long I stand there, trembling, half-lost. It could be moments, it could be hours. Time here is elastic, stretching thin. All I know is that the presence wraps me in its unseen embrace, vast and consuming, until I cannot imagine existing without it.

And then, deep in the structure's dark heart,

something answers. A pulse that isn't mine, rolling through the stone, rising up into me until I am breathless. A single thought blooms in my mind, not my own but unmistakable:

You are seen.

The words—or the feeling of them—rip through me, and my knees nearly buckle. My life, my safe little shoreline existence, has already been claimed. Whether this is gift or doom, I cannot yet tell.

But as the fire laces through me, I know this much: the heart of something ancient and terrible has noticed me, and it will not let me go. In the distance, the moss ripples as though something heavy is moving beneath it. The whisper falters—just for a breath—and in that silence, I realize I am not alone.

CHAPTER THREE

The path ahead dissolves into mist, curling tendrils of fog that writhe as though they have intent. Each step I take sends a faint tremor through the ground, the pulse of this place echoing back into my bones. The moss shifts beneath my feet, alive and aware, and I can't shake the feeling that it's listening.

The whisper I've been following falters, thinning into silence. That's when the unease sets in — a prickling crawl at the base of my neck. I turn, but there's nothing behind me, only the swaying of those translucent-leaved trees. Their veins glow faintly, pulsing, as though they're holding their breath.

The air thickens, and I swear I hear footsteps —

no, more like the drag of something heavy, keeping pace.

I whisper to myself, *"It's nothing."* But the words fall flat.

The mist coils tighter, obscuring the path. My pulse climbs. I take another step, and the ground shudders beneath me, subtle but deliberate, like something massive shifting just out of sight.

Then I hear it.

A low growl. Rumbling, guttural. Not from one direction but from everywhere at once, vibrating through the fog.

I freeze, every muscle tense.

And then it emerges.

The mist parts to reveal a mass of limbs, glistening scales refracting strange colors as it moves. Too many legs, bending at angles that defy anatomy. Its eyes burn a sickly yellow — but worse, when they fix on me, I see my own reflection swimming in them, fractured and distorted. Its mouth unfurls, rows of teeth slick with a dark sheen, dripping onto the moss, which recoils as if in pain.

The growl rises, echoing like a broken chorus.

It lunges.

I stumble backward, tripping over a root that coils like a grasping hand. The creature looms above me, its scales rasping against my skin as it pins me down. Its breath reeks of brine and rot. The glint of its teeth hovers inches from my throat.

I push against it, my arms trembling, but it's like trying to hold back a tide.

The whisper is gone.

All that remains is the thunder of my heartbeat — and the certainty that I am about to be devoured.

And then, the air changes.

CHAPTER FOUR

The atmosphere bends. The mist recoils, pulling back like a curtain. The monster above me stiffens, every limb trembling. And then *he* arrives.

He towers over us, wrought from shadow and sea. His skin gleams a dark, abyssal green, his eyes burning with light that cuts through me like a blade. Tentacles frame his face like a crown, moving with deliberate grace, alive with their own intent.

The world itself bows to him. The ground steadies beneath my back. The mist stills. Even the air vibrates in his presence.

One tentacle lashes out, wrapping the beast that pinned me. He lifts it effortlessly, ignoring its flailing limbs, its gnashing teeth. In his grasp, the creature is pathetic, a child's toy. He studies it, impassive, before casting it into the fog with a flick. The sound of its fall echoes once, then silence devours it.

And then there is only him.

My chest heaves, my pulse frantic. I should be trembling in fear. Instead, heat floods me, thick and molten. My thighs press together, desperate, and I know, I've never been this turned on in my life. He is beautiful in a way that defies explanation, a creature of darkness and mystery.

He turns his gaze on me, and the world narrows. His eyes burn into me, stripping me down to marrow, seeing every hidden hunger I've tried to bury. A shiver courses through me, but it's not dread — it's want.

"You are safe," he rumbles. The sound vibrates through my body, deep and resonant. My nipples tighten, my breath stutters. Safe is not what I feel. Claimed, undone, *seen* — yes.

A tentacle brushes my cheek. Warm, smooth, stronger than steel yet tender in its glide. My skin tingles, sparks racing down my neck. Another trails across my collarbone, dipping lower, and I gasp, arching toward him without thought.

Gods. He is terrifying. He is magnificent. And he is touching me like I belong to him.

"Who... who are you?" My voice fractures, but it isn't only fear that shakes it.

His mouth curves into a smile, sharp and dangerous.

"I am the pulse you felt in the stone," he murmurs, low and intimate. "The rhythm that claimed your heart. I am Cthulhu."

The name reverberates inside me, drumming in my chest and low in my belly. My thighs ache with the need for more.

He bends closer, tentacles sliding around my waist, pulling me against the hard plane of his chest. His strength is absolute, yet his grip is measured, coaxing. My breath comes ragged. My body is betraying me, or maybe it's finally honest, I want this nightmare. I want him.

"There is something in you," he says, his words a hot whisper against my ear. A tentacle traces my hip, curling possessively. "A hunger that matches mine. You ache for more than safety. You ache for ruin."

A whimper escapes me — needy, desperate — and I don't care.

"Tell me," he commands, his tentacle sliding lower, hovering just at the edge of where I burn for him. "Do you want me to stop?"

"No," I breathe, the truth pulled raw from my chest. "Gods, no. Don't stop."

His eyes flare, triumphant. Another tentacle curves between my thighs, pressing firmly through the thin barrier of my clothes. The contact steals my breath, heat surging up my spine. I rock against him helplessly, shamelessly.

"You crave the unknown," he growls, his words vibrating inside me as his tentacle teases slow circles against my most sensitive flesh. "You crave *me*."

"Yes," I gasp, my hips moving with his rhythm. "Please—"

He rewards me, the appendage slipping beneath fabric, finding me slick and ready. The first stroke against bare skin makes me cry out, my body arching. The world tilts, every nerve aflame, every thought consumed.

Another tentacle coils around my breast, squeezing, teasing my nipple until sparks burst behind my eyes. His grip is possessive, but every movement is deliberate, reading me, feeding my pleasure.

His grip tightens, possessive, and I should be terrified. I *am*. But terror melts into desire, a twin flame.

I close my eyes, whispering the truth I cannot deny: "I don't want to leave. I want this. I want *you*."

His smile deepens, dark and triumphant. A tentacle curls beneath my chin, tilting my face up to his.

"You already belong," he murmurs. "Did you think the ring was trinket or charm? No, little one. It was carved from my own sigil, bound to my heart. When you slipped it on, you did not choose a bauble. You chose *me*."

The words strike through me like lightning. For a moment I can't even picture Coral Cove, or Rainbow's shop, or the path I walked to get here. Those things blur, fading like dreams at dawn. Had they ever existed? Or had I always been meant to be here, waiting for him?

"This realm is not separate from me," he continues, his voice low and intimate, vibrating through my body. "Every breath of wind, every pulse beneath your feet is mine. When you walk here, you walk inside my heart. When you touch the stone, you touch *me*."

A tentacle glides down my waist, sliding between my thighs with aching precision. My gasp shatters into a moan.

"And now you wear my mark," he growls, eyes

blazing. "The ring calls you to me. It roots you here. The longer you stay, the more this place will replace what you left behind. Already you forget the shore you came from. Already you ache for nothing but me."

He's right. The thought of Coral Cove feels distant, faded, like something I read about in a story once. The ache in my chest isn't homesickness — it's him.

"Say it," he demands, his tentacles holding me in place, teasing, consuming. "Say whose you are."

"I'm yours," I moan, broken and certain. "I've always been yours." The confession ripped from me with no hesitation, no doubt. "I'm yours."

He rewards me with a deeper thrust of his touch, tentacles tightening, guiding me higher. Pleasure rips through me in waves, building fast, unstoppable.

The moss beneath me pulses with the same rhythm, amplifying every sensation until I'm drowning in him, in this world, in the fire he's lit inside me.

When the climax crashes over me, it's not just an orgasm — it's communion. My body convulses, crying out his name, the pulse of his world echoing in mine.

And through it all, his eyes hold me, dark and endless, filled with hunger and possession.

When I finally collapse against him, trembling and undone, he lowers his mouth to my ear, his tentacles still coiled tight.

"Stay," he whispers, the word both promise and threat. "Stay, and I will show you the true depths of my heart."

And gods help me — I already know I will.

CHAPTER FIVE

Cthulhu leads me deeper into his world, his massive tentacles moving with a grace that defies their size. They coil and uncoil over the glowing terrain, guiding me forward as though this entire realm bends to his will. His gaze never leaves me, ancient and hungry, eyes lit with an unearthly glow that makes my skin prickle.

Tentacles brush my shoulders, my hips, warm and deliberate. Others hover at the edges of my path, protective, directing. Their strength is undeniable, every caress a reminder that they could crush me — and yet, they handle me with startling gentleness. The duality sends shivers down my spine.

He wraps one thick tentacle around my waist

and pulls me close until I can feel the heat radiating from his body. His voice is a low growl, soft but irresistible.

"You are mine, Maddison. The ring promised me you would come. It was forged from my heart, and it brought me my queen. My goddess."

"You still cling to fragments of the shore," he murmured, his gaze piercing mine. "Your little home, the bed where you slept alone. The job where you taught tourists what you already knew, day after day, until even your passion dulled. The friends who moved on without you. The family who never saw you, not truly. Tell me, Maddison — do those scraps still feel real to you?"

My chest tightens. I try to summon their faces, their voices. My cramped apartment, the sound of the waves through my window, the clatter of seashells in my classroom bin. But the images blur, dissolving like water through my fingers. Already they feel distant, like photographs left out in the sun too long.

"All you have left," Cthulhu said, tightening his grip, "is me. And all you will ever need... is me."

The words sear through me. Queen. Goddess. The titles feel too big, too heavy — and yet they spark something buried in me, something I didn't know I'd been waiting to hear. I look into his endless, swirling eyes and see no doubt, only conviction, I was always meant to belong here. To him.

His tentacles tighten, not painfully, but with unrelenting possession. "You are not lost," he murmurs. "You are found. This realm is my body, my heart, and now it will be yours. Coral Cove? That mortal shore you once clung to?" His smile is sharp, knowing. "Already it fades. Already you forget the shop, the girl who sold you my ring. It feels like lifetimes ago, doesn't it?"

And gods — he's right. The memory of Rainbow's shop, of the boardwalk, of the gulls and the tide feels impossibly far away, like a dream I once lived. All that matters is him, this place, the rhythm I now breathe in my bones.

"You never felt at home there," he says, his gaze boring into mine, unrelenting. "Always watching, never belonging. But here?" His tentacles spread wide, encircling me. "Here, you are seen. Here, you are worshipped."

The hiss cuts through the air like a knife. From the mist, a shape uncoils, glinting wetly, scales shifting like living metal. Its jaw splits open far too wide, rows of fangs dripping venom that hisses where it hits the glowing moss.

I stumble back, my heart hammering. The creature's body keeps unfolding, too many limbs, too many eyes blinking in sickly yellow. One eye fixes on me, and I feel a wave of hatred so sharp it steals my breath.

It lunges. I scream, throwing myself sideways, barely dodging the first strike. Its claws rake the earth where I stood, sparks of blue fire erupting from the moss. I scramble, but it's fast — far too fast. Its breath hits me, rancid and wet.

I trip, falling hard. Its bulk looms over me, limbs braced on either side, venom dripping so close I can smell the acid burn. Its jaws open wide, angling for my throat—

And then the world itself shudders.

Cthulhu's roar is not sound but earthquake, rolling through my chest. Tentacles whip outward, encircling me, forcing the beast back. The ground cracks beneath his fury as he strikes. One lash sends the creature sprawling. Another coils it whole, crushing as shrieks split the air.

But Cthulhu does not hesitate. His tentacles unfurl in a protective ring, walls of living muscle surrounding me. The air vibrates with his fury. The squeeze is merciless, bones snapping, until the beast bursts into a mist of red dust that dissipates into the glowing fog.

"You dare threaten her?" Cthulhu growls, his voice a tremor that rattles the stones. His wrath is terrible, absolute. Then his gaze softens as it returns to me, scanning for fear.

His tentacles retract, hovering, stroking my arms, my shoulders. His eyes search mine, burning, relentless.

"Are you afraid of me, Maddison?"

For a moment, I hesitate. My body trembles, and gods, I *should* be. He is a monster. He just crushed something bigger than me into dust without effort. His touch alone could break me. Fear would be natural.

But when I meet his eyes, when I feel the steady heat of his tentacles stroking my skin, I know the truth.

"I should be," I whisper. "But I'm not. Not of you."

The admission pulls something raw out of me, so intimate I almost flinch at my own honesty. "I can't lie to you. I'm not afraid."

For the first time, his expression falters — not weakness, but surprise. Then hunger burns through it, fierce and possessive.

His tentacles retract, moving over my arms, my shoulders, softer now, drawing patterns of heat across my skin.

Something flickers in his expression, surprise giving way to raw hunger. His tentacles coil tighter, possessive, his body radiating heat.

"You are mine," he says again, rougher this time, his desire evident. "And I would crush this realm to ash before I let it take you from me."

The fierceness in his voice ignites something reckless inside me. I tilt my head back, meeting his burning gaze, and all I can think is *yes*.

"Yes," I whisper, breathless. "I understand."

He claims me then.

Tentacles coil around my body, lifting me effortlessly against his chest. One binds my thighs, spreading me open as another traces slowly, deliberately over the most sensitive parts of me. The first touch steals my breath. The next makes me cry out, my voice breaking into the mist.

"Here," he growls, his voice vibrating through every nerve, "I will make you mine."

His touch is everywhere, relentless and skilled — a multitude of lips, tongues, hands, all at once. Each stroke leaves fire in its wake, claiming me, awakening me. I moan his name, tangled in pleasure and fear, as his tentacles map every inch of me, wrapping tighter, drawing me deeper into his embrace.

"You are my queen," he whispers, his mouth close to my ear, a storm of heat and shadows around us. "My goddess. My ruin. And now, my consort."

The words tear through me as his caresses drive me higher, until I am nothing but fire, nothing but need. My climax rips me apart, a violent, beautiful surrender. The moss pulses with us, the air vibrates, the entire realm seems to echo my release.

And through it all, Cthulhu holds me, his tentacles binding, caressing, claiming. His eyes burn with triumph, with hunger, with a love as dark as it is terrifying.

When the world finally steadies, when I collapse against him shaking and undone, he whispers the promise I can never escape.

"Stay, Maddison. Stay, and be my queen. My goddess. Mine — for all eternity."

CHAPTER SIX

Cthulhu carried me deeper into his domain, his massive tentacles cradling me as though I were precious and fragile. The labyrinth sprawled outward endlessly, its walls bending at impossible angles, shapes twisting in ways my mind could barely hold.

This place should have overwhelmed me with fear.

But instead, it felt inevitable.

Every step, every pulsating archway we passed, every strange whispering breeze stirred something inside me. It was as if I'd been here before, as if this was where I'd always belonged.

We reached a vast chamber at the heart of the labyrinth, the walls undulating like they were breathing. Towering ruins loomed in every direction, etched with glowing sigils that pulsed in rhythm with my heartbeat. At its center stood an altar of black marble veined with molten silver.

As Cthulhu set me down, the air grew heavy, thick with energy. His tentacles coiled around my waist, my arms, my thighs, possessive yet protective. I gazed up at him, my pulse quickening. There was something different in his expression—a shadow I hadn't seen before.

He touched my face with a single tentacle, caressing me as though weighing a terrible truth. His other limbs hovered, tense and restless, like serpents sensing danger.

"There's something you're not telling me," I whispered.

His eyes, vast and ancient, darkened. "You've felt it too. The unease in this realm. The warping. The way reality bends." His voice was deeper than ever, a current pulling me under. "The weight of what you've stepped into is more than desire or fate. It is danger, Maddison."

My breath caught. "I know something is wrong. But I don't... understand it."

"You will," he rumbled, his gaze never leaving

mine. "You deserve to understand. Even if it terrifies you."

I swallowed hard. "Tell me."

He drew me close, his tentacles wrapping fully around me until I was surrounded by him, encased in heat and strength. "There is a reason why you were drawn to me—why you feel as though you've always known me."

I clutched at him, needing to hear the truth even as I feared it.

"You and I are bound," he said, each word heavy with sorrow. "Not just here, not just now, but across countless lifetimes. Every time you are born, every time you return, you find me. And each time, you are torn from me."

A chill swept over me. "Torn from you?"

"Yes." His voice deepened, a growl of rage beneath the grief. "There is another. A force of chaos older than your world, older than the seas and stars. It despises what we are. It claims that nothing should be mine. That no one should belong to me."

His tentacles trembled around me, as though holding back a storm.

"The first time you came to me, it tried to destroy us," he continued. "When it failed, it cursed you. Now, in every life, it finds you. It rips you away, destroys you, and leaves me to wait. And every time you return, I must fight to keep you."

Tears burned my eyes. The weight of it crashed into me—lifetimes of love and loss, over and over again.

"This... this thing," I stammered. "It's coming now, isn't it?"

"Yes." His eyes glowed like twin suns. "Even now, it feels our bond. The closer it comes, the more this realm shatters beneath its touch. The shifting you've seen, the instability—it is the shadow of its arrival."

I shivered, both from fear and from the way his tentacles tightened around me, protective, unyielding.

"What do we do?" I whispered.

"We prepare," he vowed. "I will fight it, as I have fought before. But this time..." His voice dropped lower, intimate and fierce. "This time, it will not take you from me."

His words hung in the air like a vow etched into the bones of the realm. My breath came fast, chest heaving as my heart pounded in a rhythm that no longer felt entirely my own. Fear curled inside me, sharp and cold, but it was tangled with something hotter, deeper—a fierce yearning that burned brighter than the terror.

Images flickered at the edges of my mind: my cramped apartment, the salt-and-coffee smell of the Maritime Center, familiar faces of friends and family. They were hazy, distant, like paintings smeared by water. I tried to cling to them, to remember the sound of my own world... but the memories slipped through my fingers like sand.

And then there was *him*.

Cthulhu's tentacles stroked my skin, steady and warm, anchoring me to the present—*to him*. His eyes held me, unblinking, ancient, filled with a hunger that saw every secret place inside me and claimed it.

The more I looked at him, the less those blurred images mattered. My old life wasn't just fading; it was becoming unreal, like a story I'd been told once but never lived.

"Then let us bind ourselves tighter," he murmured, his voice shifting from warlord to lover, fierce to devastatingly tender. "Before the void comes, I will make certain you are wholly mine— body, heart, and soul. No force will tear you from me if you are woven into the very heart of this realm."

His words struck something deep inside me. For

the first time, I understood: this wasn't just about protection or survival. This was about belonging.

I trembled, not from fear, but from the enormity of what I felt—for him, for us. If the world I came from was already dissolving, why keep grasping for it? Why fight for something that had never truly been mine when here, now, he was offering me everything?

As the darkness of his domain curled closer, enclosing us like a living cocoon, I knew with absolute certainty: I didn't just want him to claim me. I *wanted to claim him back*. To be his, completely and irrevocably, before the chaos could come between us.

He laid me back on the black marble altar. The stone was cold beneath my spine, stark against the fevered heat of his touch.

"You are mine," he said, his voice a vibration in the very air. "This realm is mine, and you are its queen. Its goddess. My heart made flesh."

His tentacles moved slowly, reverently, sliding beneath my clothes, peeling them away piece by piece. Cool air kissed my skin, followed by the hot, deliberate path of his touch.

As he revealed me, I reached for him in return, my fingers tracing his dark green skin. It was rough and smooth at once, ridges and suctions pulsing gently beneath my touch. He shuddered under my hands, a low rumble of approval echoing through the chamber.

"Maddison," he groaned, his voice a plea and a command all at once.

The tentacles moved like living tongues, tasting me, kissing every inch of my skin. My breath hitched, my body arching. The world narrowed to the intimate cocoon of the ruins, reality warping around us.

"You belong to no mortal shore," he said, his tentacle circling my throat lightly, possessively. "Not to the home you once clung to. Not to your bed, your job, your family who never truly saw you. Those ties are gone. Here, with me, you are eternal."

His words dissolved the last threads of my old life. My apartment, my students, the sound of gulls —all blurred into unreality. All that existed was him.

One tentacle wrapped around my waist, lifting me. Another brushed over my lips, teasing, tasting.

My mouth opened in answer, my tongue exploring him, the textured surface both alien and addicting. His growl of pleasure reverberated through me as I took him deeper, worshipping him as he worshipped me.

His other tentacles slid over my body, teasing, claiming. One found my clit, the suction flickering in maddening patterns that made me cry out. Another coiled around my breast, tugging at my nipple. A third wrapped lightly around my throat, a reminder of his control.

And then he filled me.

The stretch was shocking, exquisite. He paused to let me adjust, his eyes watching mine for consent. I nodded desperately, wanting more.

Each thrust was a wave, a tide crashing over me. My cries echoed off the ancient walls, mingling with his low, guttural growls.

"You are mine," he growled, pounding into me with a rhythm that matched the pulse of this realm. "Say it."

"I'm yours!" I screamed, my body shattering around him. "Always yours!"

Pleasure consumed me, raw and endless. My climax tore through me like a cosmic storm, shaking the very ground. His tentacles held me steady as he followed me over the edge, releasing inside me with a flood of heat that felt like it branded me from the inside out.

When it was over, he cradled me against his chest. His tentacles were softer now, stroking me gently, rocking me as if to soothe me back from the edge of oblivion.

"Rest, my queen," he murmured, his voice tender but edged with darkness. "While you can."

I blinked up at him, exhausted. "While I can?"

His gaze flickered toward the shifting walls. "The void stirs. The enemy comes closer. Soon, this realm will not be safe."

A chill slid through me. But his arms were warm, his embrace absolute.

And in that moment, fear didn't matter.

Nothing mattered but him.

As sleep pulled me under, his last words followed me into the darkness:

"You are mine, Maddison. And I will tear the stars apart before I let them take you again."

CHAPTER SEVEN

In the sanctum of Cthulhu's otherworldly domain, time was no longer a constant.

It ebbed and flowed like a tide with no moon to guide it, surging forward one moment and pulling back the next. Sometimes hours seemed to stretch into eternities. Other times, days—or weeks, maybe even years—vanished in the blink of an eye.

I would catch glimpses of another life at odd moments, a cluttered desk scattered with shells, the smell of salt and coffee in the morning, my sister's laughter carried on a distant breeze. The sound of tourists on the boardwalk, a warm hand in mine, a familiar blue mug resting on the counter.

But every time I reached for those memories, they blurred and melted away like water through cupped hands. Faces became smudges. Names dissolved. Even my own reflection felt foreign, unreal.

Only this realm remained sharp and vivid.

Only *him*.

Reality bent beneath Cthulhu's ancient magic. The walls of the sanctum breathed like living things, their surfaces rippling with luminous veins. Shadows shifted like tides, stretching and contracting in unnatural rhythms. My body felt their pull, as though my heartbeat had been rewritten to match this place's strange, unearthly pulse.

The ruins surrounding us seemed alive.

Each archway whispered, each stone throbbed faintly, as though they were all connected to a single, vast consciousness. It was terrifying. It was beautiful. And somehow, I knew I was now part of it.

———

CTHULHU STOOD BEFORE ME, a towering silhouette that blotted out what faint light the ruins provided. He was larger here than he had ever seemed, his tentacles draped like living banners, his body vast enough to cast shadows that swallowed entire walls.

When he looked at me, my knees weakened. When he touched me, my doubts faltered.

But today, there was something different in his gaze. Hunger, yes, but also tenderness and an almost unbearable sorrow. A weight older than time itself.

"You've always been mine, Maddison," he said, his voice a deep rumble that reverberated through the stone beneath my feet. "In every lifetime, we find each other. Your soul has always known where it belongs."

A shiver tore through me. His words didn't just sound true—they *were* true, ringing inside me like a song I'd always known but forgotten how to sing.

Images flickered in my mind, sharp and vivid, each one crashing into me like a wave.

A battlefield stretched before me, crimson and burning. Smoke choked the air, and beneath it all was the thunderous sound of his roar. His massive form loomed above me, terrible and magnificent, while I stood drenched in sweat and blood, a sword clutched tightly in my hand. The blade dripped red, proof of a war I couldn't remember fighting, and yet somehow, I *knew* I had fought for him.

The scene dissolved, replaced by a temple draped in silks and firelight. My body knelt before him, painted in intricate, sacred runes that shimmered against my skin. His tentacles brushed my bowed head with a reverence that made my chest ache, and I felt the weight of worship—of belonging—settle over me like a crown.

Another vision surged forward: a throne of bone and gold rising high above a crowd that trembled in terror. He sat upon it, dark and all-powerful, while one tentacle curled possessively around my hand. My head was held high as I stood beside him, a queen feared and adored in equal measure.

And then came the most devastating image of all—my own face. Over and over again, changing with the passage of centuries. Different hair, different clothes, different lives. But always *me*, always gazing up at him with awe, love, and an unshakable recognition.

I gasped, stumbling back as the visions shattered, leaving me breathless beneath their weight.

Cthulhu's tentacles slid over my skin in slow, deliberate movements, grounding me in the present. His touch was no longer just desire—it was ritual, remembrance, a sealing of a bond that stretched beyond lifetimes.

"I have held you as a warrior drenched in blood," he murmured, his voice soft but inexorable. "As a priestess crowned in flame. As a queen draped in gold and sorrow. I have found you in every world, every age. And every time you are torn from me, I hunt the stars until you are reborn."

One tentacle curled beneath my chin, tilting my face up toward his. His gaze burned with fury and love.

"But this time, Maddison... this time, the void itself hungers for you. And I will not lose you again."

Two tentacles wrapped around my wrists, firm but not painful. My body yielded instinctively, trusting him. It wasn't restraint born of fear. It was surrender, complete and willing.

"Cthulhu," I breathed, my voice shaking. His touch roamed lower, reverent and possessive, trailing over my ribs, my hips, tracing every curve like he was relearning me.

"I feel like I've known you forever," I admitted. "But I'm afraid..."

He stilled, his form going unnaturally still. A single tentacle slid beneath my chin, lifting my gaze to his.

"You fear losing yourself," he said, voice low and unearthly gentle. "You fear that by staying with me, you will become something else."

The words struck so deeply that for a moment, I couldn't breathe.

Because it was true.

My skin felt different beneath his touch, my heartbeat syncing to his rhythm. My thoughts sometimes slipped into his cadence, my dreams merging with memories that weren't mine.

I tried to summon the face of someone I'd loved once. My sister, my best friend. Even my own name whispered on their lips.

Nothing came.

Only him.

Was I Maddison—the girl who once taught children about sea stars and tidal pools? Or was I something new now? Something his?

"I should fight this," I whispered, trembling. "But I... I don't want to."

His tentacles tightened, surrounding me completely, a living cage of heat and velvet strength.

"You've already given yourself to me," he murmured. "And I have given myself to you. We are bound—across time, across realms. That bond will never fade, even if you tried to leave."

The admission shattered the last fragile walls I'd built.

Desire surged through me, raw and consuming.

His tentacles moved again, slow and deliberate, tracing fire over my skin. Every touch was precise, devastating, peeling me apart layer by layer. My breath came in gasps as he mapped every sensitive place, every secret need, every hidden ache.

The cool, textured surface of his skin contrasted with the searing heat of his passion. One tentacle circled my throat lightly, possessive but not constricting—a reminder of his power, of how easily he could take or give breath. Another teased between my thighs, coaxing sounds from me I didn't recognize as my own.

"You are mine," he growled, his voice dark silk.

"Say it."

"I'm yours!" The words tore from me, raw and reverent. "Always yours!"

His answering roar shook the chamber, a sound of triumph and possession that reverberated through my bones. For a heartbeat, the world went still, balanced on the edge of something vast and dangerous. His tentacles tightened around me, holding me as though to seal my vow into the very marrow of my being. I felt his power sink deeper, twining with mine, until I couldn't tell where I ended and he began.

Then the rhythm of his touch shifted. Pleasure

crested higher, sharper. The ruins around us pulsed in response, their veins glowing brighter, the walls bending into impossible shapes.

I arched beneath him, body trembling on the edge of ecstasy and destruction. He pushed me to my very limits, and just when I thought I would shatter, he pulled me back, whispering commands that anchored me in place.

"Breathe," he commanded.

And somehow, I did.

Each thrust, each stroke built into something vast, something terrifying. The air shimmered, filled with maddening whispers. It wasn't just the two of us anymore—this entire realm watched, rejoiced, *joined* in our union.

Then, beneath the harmony, I heard something else.

A sound colder, deeper.

A note of discord that didn't belong.

The ruins shuddered.

A shadow split across the far wall like a crack in glass.

For a heartbeat, I felt *another gaze*—alien, ravenous, furious.

The void was watching.

My climax ripped through me like a tidal wave,

obliterating thought. I screamed his name, my body breaking apart under the force of it. Cthulhu roared in answer, his tentacles locking around me as he poured himself into me, claiming me completely.

The walls rippled violently, light flaring and dimming as if reality itself couldn't contain what we'd done.

Then, just as suddenly, silence fell.

I collapsed against him, sobbing, my limbs trembling. His tentacles stroked my skin, softer now, gentle and soothing. He gathered me into his chest, cradling me like something fragile and infinitely precious.

"You are mine, Maddison," he whispered, his voice a promise etched in blood and eternity. "Always."

As sleep dragged at me, I caught a flicker of movement beyond him—a pale, writhing shape that vanished when I blinked.

The harmony of the ruins hummed uneasily. Somewhere in the distance, a low, guttural sound rose.

The void was closer now.

Cthulhu's arms tightened around me, and his voice followed me into the dark.

"Rest, my queen. For soon, nothing will be safe."

CHAPTER EIGHT

The air was wrong.

It pressed against my skin like damp velvet, humming with a low current that rode beneath my heartbeat. Shadows clung to the edges of the ruins and twitched when I wasn't looking straight at them. Hairline cracks veined the cyclopean stones, weeping threads of black light that looked like ink suspended in water. When I drew a breath, my lungs burned, as if the atmosphere itself objected to me being here.

Something was coming, and the realm knew it.

I stood beside Cthulhu, his towering form throwing a darkness that swallowed the ruins' faint glow. He was my anchor; without him the ground felt tilted, the geometry untrustworthy. Once, the impossible angles and breathing walls had terrified me. Now their pulse matched my own. I couldn't tell where I ended and this place began.

Comfort was not the same as safety.

His eyes were on me—always watching, always weighing. Possession still burned there, but beneath it moved something gentler and heavier: tenderness, sorrow, an old grief that made my chest ache to look at. It scared me more than his power ever had. If he could feel, he could be hurt.

"You are mine," he had told me, and I had believed him. Lately a different truth had been threading itself through my thoughts: perhaps, somehow, he was becoming mine too.

Part of me longed to drown in him, to let his tentacles draw quiet maps across my skin until there was nothing left to name but us. Another part—the one that remembered tide pools and sun-warmed boards and gulls carving the sky—whispered that staying would mean forgetting. Not just faces and places, but the shape of the person who had loved them.

"Your mind is loud today," he rumbled, the sound settling through the stone and into my bones. A warm band of muscle brushed my forearm, and I shivered. "What troubles you, my queen?"

I hesitated. To lie to him felt impossible.

"Everything feels... uncertain," I said. "I belong here with you. I feel it. But something's changing. I can feel that, too. And it scares me."

For an instant his vast form went very still. A shadow passed through his expression like a cloud over a moon. His tentacles tightened around my waist, protective, then loosened as if he feared his own strength.

"The world is changing," he said at last. "Forces have woken—old, jealous things. They see what we have made and would rather unmake it than let you remain by my side."

A chill moved through me. "What are they?"

"They were the architects of nightmares," he said, and his eyes darkened until they seemed bottomless. "When this realm was young, they bent reality to their will. They fed on panic and ruin, twisted worlds into screaming voids. I shattered them once—or believed I had. But remnants linger. Hungry. Waiting."

The ruins groaned softly, as if in answer. A fresh fissure opened along the nearest wall with a dry crack and bled a little more black light.

His grip firmed. "And now they have scented

you. My heart. My queen. They cannot hurt me as I am; they will hurt me through you."

The word heart struck something deep and unsteady inside me. For a heartbeat, Coral Cove rose up bright and close: the slap of waves against the pier, sunscreen and coffee, a little blue mug chipped at the rim, my sister's laughter like a gull's cry. I turned toward the sound—toward that unassuming, human life—and watched it dissolve into mist, leaving only the alien glow of the sanctum and his heat at my back.

"Then when they come," I asked, voice low, "what happens if they succeed?"

"They will not." His promise shook the air. "I will tear down every shadow, every star, every whisper that dares touch you."

But as he said it, the edges of him flickered like heat above asphalt, a stutter that wasn't there before. The sight threaded a new fear through the old ones. He had seemed unbreakable. Now I could see where the world tugged at him.

"Tell me what to do," I said. "Tell me how to help."

His eyes softened, the old grief rising again. "There is only one choice that protects you." The great limbs around me eased, not retreating, only gentling. When he spoke, the command in his voice had thinned to something quieter and more fragile. "You must leave."

For a moment I couldn't find breath enough to answer. The word didn't fit in my mouth. "Leave?"

"You could go back," he said carefully, as if each syllable were a blade he had to carry across his own tongue. "Back to your soft tides and mortal years. Back to a life that does not know this war. There, you would be beyond their reach."

"And you?"

"I remain," he said simply. "I hold what I can. I fight as I have always fought." His form shimmered again, then steadied. "If you leave..." A pause. A fracture. "You will take a part of me with you."

Tears burned hot and sudden. "I don't want to leave you. I don't want to lose this."

"You will not lose me," he said, cupping my face with a palm the size of a shield, tender as rain. "Death has not kept me from you. Emptiness has not kept me. When it is safe, when the void is quiet again, I will find you."

The ground shuddered hard enough to stagger me. He caught me before I could fall, wrapping me in a cage of living warmth. Cold rushed across the floor like a tide drawing back from shore. From the cracks, mist rose—not like weather, but like breath from a mouth just beyond the veil. Shapes moved within it. Too many eyes opened and closed in perfect unison. Pale limbs slid along the edge of sight and withdrew. A thousand voices whispered in reverse, and inside the chorus I heard my own name, layered over itself, calling from a distance I could not measure.

"They are coming," he said, and the edges of his voice sharpened. "The chaos will not wait."

"I don't know what to do," I said, and hated how small I sounded.

"You will know," he answered, fierce and certain as a tide. "When the moment comes, you will know."

The fissure behind him widened with a wet crack. The black light inside pulsed like a dying heartbeat. I stared into it and felt something stare back, cold and eager. The air thinned. The sanctum's glow guttered. Stones popped like cooling metal.

"Tell me how to go," I whispered.

"When I tell you," he said, every word deliberate, "listen for the rhythm that is not your own. Turn your ring to that beat. Step where the air feels thinner. The door will find you."

Another tremor rolled through the chamber,

stronger than before. The mist thickened, grew teeth. It pressed against us like a crowd. The reverse-whispers built into a wet, ululating hum that made my teeth ache. A thin, taloned shadow pushed at the fissure until the stone around it bowed inward. The seam tore open the width of a hand, then a forearm, then wider, spilling a smear of night into the room.

"Back," he snarled, and the room seemed to obey him for a breath. The shadows flinched. The hum faltered. He drew himself to his full, impossible height, tentacles unfurling in an arc around me, his body interposed between me and the crack.

He looked down at me once, the universe crowding behind his eyes. For the first time since I had slipped the ring onto my finger on a bright afternoon by an ordinary sea, I saw fear there. Not for himself.

For me.

"We are out of time," he said.

The seam screamed wider. Something vast pressed through—slick and pale, studded with eyes that opened like wounds. The temperature dropped; my breath plumed. The ringing in my ears became a howl.

Cthulhu wrapped me tight and shoved me behind the curve of his body. His roar broke over the chamber, the sound of trenches groaning under continents.

"Run," he commanded, voice splitting the world.

I reached for him instead.

"Maddison," he said, not looking back, every limb braced against the thing forcing its way through, "choose."

The crack vomited night.

The floor bucked. The ruins' pulse stuttered.

And with the enemy's first limb spilling into the sanctum and Cthulhu standing against it like a storm-torn cliff, I understood that whatever choice I made in the next breath would break something—my heart, this realm, or the last thin thread tying me to the shore I used to call home.

CHAPTER NINE

The world trembled beneath my feet.

For days, I had felt it building—a tension that clung to my skin like oil and seeped into my lungs with every breath. The air tasted of ash and metal, acrid and sharp, and each inhale burned as if the very atmosphere wanted me gone. Shadows no longer lay still. They twitched and stretched, clawing at the edges of the ruins like living things trying to escape.

Beneath it all, there was a pulse.

Faint at first, like a second heartbeat just under the surface.

Now it throbbed so violently it rattled my bones, a rhythm that didn't match my own.

The realm itself was screaming in silence.

The stones beneath my feet cracked in slow, jagged lines that glowed faintly before bleeding black mist. Above, the sky twisted, streaks of violet and green warping into spirals, then collapsing back into a void so deep it hurt to look at. The ruins seemed to groan under invisible weight, their impossible angles bending into shapes that threatened to tear my mind apart if I stared too long.

Something vast and hungry pressed against this world.

And it was pushing harder with every passing second.

Cthulhu had been silent for hours.

His tentacles still wrapped around my waist, still brushed against my shoulders, but the touches were different now. Not teasing, not seductive—protective and heavy, as though he were already bracing for the inevitable. His great body thrummed with contained power, muscles shifting beneath his dark, scaled skin, ready to strike.

I reached up, resting my trembling hand on one of the warm, smooth bands of muscle encircling me. It trembled faintly. Not from fear—Cthulhu was never afraid—but from the sheer, restless force inside him, a tidal wave waiting to be unleashed. His eyes burned brighter than ever before, twin abysses glowing with the weight of eons, but beneath the fury, I saw it: worry.

Ancient, impossible worry for *me*.

The sight stole my breath.

Before I could speak, the sky *split open*.

No warning. No rumble of thunder or flash of lightning. Just a violent *ripping*, like the sound of a thousand sails tearing at once. A jagged wound appeared above us, slashing across the horizon.

From that wound, darkness poured forth.

It wasn't natural darkness—it was thick and alive, a crawling, writhing substance that devoured the faint light of the ruins as it spread. It bled into the cracks, smothered the glowing veins beneath the stone, and curled upward like smoke choking the sky. Where it passed, color died, leaving only gray and sickly pallor in its wake.

My heart stuttered.

I didn't have to see what emerged to know that *this* was what had been pressing against the world all along.

And then I saw it.

At first, it was only a ripple in the dark, a disturbance like heat on asphalt. Then it stepped forward, and reality *shuddered* around it.

It wasn't a creature.

It was a *presence*, an idea made flesh, a walking blasphemy of form.

Limbs emerged and dissolved, bending at wrong angles, some moving too fast while others jerked too slow, as if they existed in different timelines altogether. Too many eyes bloomed across its surface like pale, lidless flowers, opening and closing in unison before winking out again. Every time I tried to focus, my vision blurred, my mind recoiling like it was being burned.

It didn't *belong* to this world—or to any world.

Cthulhu's power had always felt like the ocean: vast, ancient, relentless.

This was different.

This was annihilation given shape.

My legs locked. Breath tore from my lungs in short, panicked gasps. Every instinct screamed at me to run, to *hide*, but my body wouldn't move. My muscles refused to obey, frozen by a terror so complete it was almost holy.

Cthulhu surged forward, shielding me with his massive form. His tentacles spread wide, forming a living barrier between me and the nightmare seeping into our world.

"Stay behind me," he commanded, his voice a guttural rumble that cracked the stone beneath us.

His tone left no room for argument, no space for fear.

The temperature plummeted. My breath crystallized white in the air.

Then it *spoke*.

The sound wasn't a voice. It was a violation. A vibration that slithered into my skull and scraped against my thoughts, reshaping them. I gagged, clutching my head, but there was no blocking it out.

"Cthulhu," it intoned, my name embedded like a splinter in the sound. "You cannot protect her. She does not belong to you."

Cthulhu's tentacles flexed, muscles coiling with rage.

"She belongs to *herself*," he snarled, his voice like a storm breaking the horizon. "And you will not have her."

The thing laughed.

The sound was worse than silence. A metallic screech, like knives grinding together, like a bone being split down the middle. My ears rang with it, and tears of pain welled in my eyes.

"She is mine by right," it hissed, each word vibrating through the ground. "You cannot keep her. You cannot even keep *yourself*."

It lunged.

The darkness surged forward like a flood unleashed.

It hit Cthulhu with a force that split the sky wide open, sending shockwaves rippling through the ruins. The ground screamed beneath us, twisting into shapes that defied logic.

I was thrown backward like a rag doll. My body hit the stone hard, the breath knocked out of me. The air thickened, heavy as water, dragging at my limbs as I tried to rise.

Cthulhu roared. The sound was so loud it seemed to come from everywhere at once, rattling the bones of the world. His tentacles lashed out, striking with impossible strength, each blow shaking the realm itself.

But the darkness didn't fall back.

It *clung*. It *consumed*.

It wrapped around him like a living shroud, smothering his glow. Pale eyes blinked open inside its depths, their light burning into my retinas. Its tendrils clawed at his tentacles, tearing, pulling, suffocating.

For the first time, I saw Cthulhu falter.

His great body buckled beneath the onslaught. His form flickered like a candle flame in a violent wind, pieces of him phasing in and out of existence. The sight made something inside me shatter.

"Cthulhu!" I screamed, crawling toward him. My hands scraped against the rough stone, blood streaking my palms. The oppressive weight of their power pressed me flat, every breath a battle.

The chaos turned its gaze on me.

It wasn't just looking at me.

It was *inside* me.

My own voice whispered my name in a dozen overlapping pitches. Memories I hadn't thought about in years surfaced and scattered like broken glass: my sister's laughter, the salty tang of ocean air, the chipped rim of my favorite mug. And then they weren't mine anymore. They were *its*. It rearranged them like a cruel child pulling wings off a fly.

My stomach heaved. Tears blurred my vision.

"She is mine," it said, and this time the word didn't pass through the air. It bloomed *inside me*, a dark, slick presence winding through my veins.

I screamed, clapping my hands over my ears. It did nothing. The sound wasn't external—it was a thought made manifest.

"No," I gasped. "No, I'm not yours!"

Cthulhu's roar split the air, violent and raw.

With a surge of impossible strength, he tore free of the darkness's grip. His tentacles flared wide, striking in a sweeping arc that sent the chaos staggering back.

The chamber filled with blinding light.

But when it cleared, I saw the truth.

Cthulhu was fading.

His edges blurred, his form flickering like a dying star. I could *see through him*, through the being who had once seemed unshakable. My heart nearly broke at the sight.

"Maddison!"

My name was a ragged plea.

"You need to leave."

I shook my head, stumbling forward. "I can't leave you like this!"

"You *must!*" His voice thundered, shaking entire pillars into rubble. Beneath the command, there was desperation. A plea he couldn't hide.

"If you stay, we will *both* be destroyed. This world is tearing apart. I cannot hold it together."

The ground split beneath my feet, jagged fissures opening as black mist surged upward. Its cold touch slid over my skin, trying to drag me down. I screamed, clutching at the stone, barely keeping my balance.

"I promised to protect you," Cthulhu said, his tone suddenly soft—broken. "And I will. But you need to *survive*."

Tears streamed down my face.

Leaving meant saving myself.

Leaving meant condemning him.

"I can't," I sobbed. "Please, don't ask me to—"

"You are my heart," he growled, his tentacles trembling as they held back the chaos. "Live, Maddison. *Live so I can find you again*."

The void surged forward, its many limbs reaching for me.

Cthulhu turned, tentacles lashing, wrapping around the darkness, dragging it back.

He roared, the sound pure defiance. "Maddison! Now!"

My hands shook violently as I reached for the ring. The band that had brought me here, that bound me to him. It felt different now—colder, heavier. Alive.

Taking it off would sever our bond forever.

Behind me, the world cracked and screamed.

Before me, Cthulhu's form flickered like it was unraveling, like he was already half gone.

"I'll come back," I whispered, my voice breaking. "I swear I'll find you."

His head turned toward me, just enough for me to see his eyes—dark, endless, filled with a love that hurt to look at.

"Go," he commanded.

I slipped the ring free.

The instant it left my skin, the connection *snapped*.

Pain ripped through me, sharp and total. I screamed, clutching my chest, as if my very soul had been torn in two.

The last thing I saw was Cthulhu's form surrounded by darkness, his tentacles spread wide as he held back the void. His roar filled the chamber, an ancient vow carried on a tide of rage and love.

The world went white.

I fell through cold and silence, tumbling end over end. The taste of salt and blood clung to my tongue. For one breathless moment, I glimpsed him through the closing tear—fighting alone against a darkness that wanted to devour everything.

And then the tear sealed shut, cutting him away from me forever.

CHAPTER TEN

The moment the ring slipped free, the world **screamed**.

The sound wasn't air or stone or flesh —it was *everything* crying out at once. The sky split open in jagged cracks of light and shadow, the ruins twisting violently as if trying to wrench themselves apart. My vision fractured, breaking into shards like a shattered mirror.

Cthulhu's roar split the chaos, a sound so raw it nearly stopped my heart.

"Maddison!"

His voice was distant and too close all at once, echoing inside my skull even as the world between us unraveled. I reached for him instinctively, my fingers clawing at the air, but there was nothing to hold on to. Nothing solid.

The ground was gone.

The air was gone.

I was gone.

I FLOATED IN WHITE NOTHINGNESS, weightless and trembling. Cold bit into me, sharp and merciless, while heat surged beneath my skin where his tentacles had once held me. I couldn't tell where my body ended and the void began. My heartbeat stuttered, then synced, painfully, to a rhythm that wasn't mine.

And then I *saw* him.

Cthulhu loomed through the collapsing fragments of his world, a massive silhouette surrounded by writhing darkness. His tentacles lashed in wide, sweeping arcs, striking against the void creature as it surged forward, its limbs bending and glitching in impossible ways.

The entity's many eyes glared through the rift, pale and hungry. Its mouth—or what passed for one —opened, releasing a vibration that tore through me like claws raking my insides.

"She will never return to you," it hissed, and though the sound was not speech, I *understood*.

"She is mine. She is *chaos*."

Cthulhu roared in answer, the sound shaking even the nothingness where I drifted. "You will not touch her!"

His eyes found mine through the shattering world, and my breath caught. They were filled with everything—love, rage, desperation, and a vow so ancient it burned. He fought not just to survive, but to keep *me* safe, even as his form flickered, his edges breaking apart like mist in the wind.

PAIN WRACKED me as the bond between us tore.

It was like my soul was being peeled away layer by layer. Memories ripped through me in flashes: his touch, his voice rumbling against my skin, his world's pulsing glow, the first time he had wrapped his tentacles around me and called me *queen*.

And beneath it all, a deeper truth rose—our life-times together.

Visions surged, crashing through me in jagged flashes of memory and emotion.

I saw myself standing at his side on a towering throne of bone and gold. The air around us shimmered with heat and the cries of a thousand unseen voices. His tentacles coiled possessively around my waist, a living crown upon his throne, while the masses below bowed in terror and reverence. His gaze burned into me—not as a monster, but as a king whose entire realm existed for this moment.

The scene dissolved into a temple lit by firelight, the air thick with incense and ancient power. My body was painted in intricate runes, glowing softly against my skin as I knelt before him. The firelight danced over his massive form, casting shadows that seemed to worship him as much as I did. His tentacle brushed against my bowed head with a reverence so tender it brought tears to my eyes, binding me to him in a vow older than language.

Then the vision twisted, sharp and violent. I was gripping his hand—smaller then, mortal, fragile— as a battlefield burned around us. The sky was black with smoke and ash, the ground slick with blood. His roar rose above the chaos, a promise of vengeance, while I screamed defiance into the storm. We fought together, side by side, until the very earth split beneath us.

And through it all, one truth remained.

My own face, shifting and reshaping through lifetimes—different hair, different clothes, different ages—but always me. Always looking up at him with awe, love, and unshakable recognition. Across centuries, across worlds, across death itself, I was his.

I screamed, the sound swallowed by the void.

The pull grew stronger.

A violent force yanked me backward, dragging me away from him.

"No!" I thrashed, kicking against the nothingness, trying to reach him. "I can't leave you!"

His tentacles lashed toward me, stretching, straining, catching me around the wrist for a single, breathless instant.

"Maddison!" His voice cracked, not with command, but with grief.

"I will find you again. Across realms, across lifetimes—I *will* find you!"

"Don't let go!" I sobbed, clutching at him with everything I had.

The darkness surged between us like a tidal wave. His grip slipped.

For one heartbeat, his eyes locked with mine.

For one heartbeat, there was only us.

And then he was gone.

I was hurled backward, the force so intense it stole my scream. The last thing I saw was Cthulhu, his massive form surrounded by shadow, his roar echoing as the void swallowed him whole.

The whiteness expanded, filling everything.

My body tumbled endlessly, weightless and falling.

Then there was nothing but cold and silence.

CHAPTER ELEVEN

The moment the ring left my finger, the world around me **shattered**.

Cthulhu's roar still echoed in my mind as everything fractured—alien skies breaking like stained glass, the impossible geometry of the ruins splintering into jagged shards, and his massive, dark form collapsing into pieces that dissolved into nothingness. It all fell away at once, as though his entire realm had never been real.

I was weightless, suspended between two realities, as if caught in the space between waking and dreaming. For a heartbeat, there was no up or down, no breath or body, only white light and the hollow ache of something vital being ripped from me.

Then I was *falling*.

Cold air slammed into me like a wall.

The strange, living warmth of his world—the pulse of magic and shadow, the heartbeat I had matched my own to—was gone, replaced by something achingly ordinary: the salt-tang of sea breeze, the distant cries of gulls, the rhythmic crash of waves.

My feet hit solid ground, and I stumbled, almost collapsing under my own weight. The world righted itself beneath me, but it felt **wrong**, too small and fragile after everything I'd seen.

Coral Cove stretched out before me just as I'd left it: the familiar shoreline, the quaint buildings with sun-bleached paint, the endless roll of blue-gray sea. But to my eyes, it was as if someone had turned the saturation down. The vibrant, impossible colors of Cthulhu's realm still clung to the edges of my vision, ghostly afterimages I couldn't blink away.

The soft warmth of his tentacles, the ever-present whisper of his power—they were gone.

In their place was silence. Ordinary, human silence.

I sucked in a shaky breath. The salt air filled my lungs, grounding me, but it wasn't enough. It could never be enough.

It was over.

I was home.

And nothing would ever be the same.

The sounds of the boardwalk drifted toward me: laughter, clinking glasses, the hum of quiet conversations. A breeze stirred the seagrass, carrying the faint smell of fried food and sunscreen. Sunlight dappled the sand, warm against my skin.

All of it felt muted, distant.

As if I were watching life through a pane of glass, present but untouchable.

I wrapped my arms around myself, trying to hold in the hollow ache that had taken root deep in my chest. The cool air brushed over my skin, but it did nothing to soothe me.

The connection was gone.

The magic. The danger. The overwhelming, all-consuming intensity of his world.

All gone.

And yet... not completely.

I still felt him. A faint, stubborn echo thrumming beneath my skin, like the ghost of a heartbeat that refused to fade.

My gaze dropped to the ring cradled in my palm.

The silver band gleamed faintly in the afternoon light, heavier than any piece of jewelry had a right to be. It carried the weight of an entire world.

The stone at its center, once alive with shifting colors, now lay dull and opaque, its glow extinguished. But when I closed my hand around it, I felt it—a tiny, steady pulse.

Faint. Distant. But alive.

A promise.

I moved slowly toward the water's edge, the cool sand shifting beneath my bare feet. The sea stretched out before me, endless and calm, a flat expanse of blue-gray that seemed almost insultingly still.

I stood there for a long moment, staring out at the horizon.

Here was home.

Here were the sounds and sights I'd grown up with—the rhythmic waves, the soft cries of seabirds, the way the evening sun turned the surface of the ocean into scattered gold.

But no matter how familiar it was, I couldn't shake the feeling that *something was missing*.

The vastness of Cthulhu's realm had spoiled me for this small, contained world. His voice had drowned out every other sound. His touch had remade me.

And now he was gone.

I curled my fingers tightly around the ring until

the metal bit into my skin.

His world had been dangerous, chaotic, filled with forces that wanted to destroy me.

And yet, it had also been beautiful—terrible and breathtaking all at once.

The bond we'd shared...

It had felt like destiny.

Older than me.

Older than him.

Older than anything.

My throat tightened. The ache in my chest threatened to swallow me whole.

I had made the right choice.

I *knew* that.

The chaos that had tried to consume us was real. It would have destroyed everything—both our worlds, both our lives. Cthulhu had been right: I needed to survive, even if survival meant tearing myself away from him.

But knowing didn't make it hurt any less.

I turned the ring over in my fingers. The stone remained dark, but beneath its silence I felt that faint, defiant pulse.

Not gone.

Not severed.

Just sleeping.

"This isn't the end," I whispered, voice trembling.

The words were almost lost beneath the ocean's roar, but I didn't care. I knew he would hear them. Somewhere. Somehow.

"When you call for me again..." My throat ached, but I forced the vow out. "I'll be ready."

The wind caught my voice, carrying it out across the water.

For a moment, I let myself imagine it reaching him—threading through realms, cutting across the vast nothingness, whispering in his ear as he fought to return to me.

My eyes fluttered closed, and for a heartbeat, I *felt* him.

Warmth against my skin.

A deep, steady presence that could never truly be gone.

Watching. Waiting. Wanting.

When I opened my eyes, the feeling faded, leaving only the ache and the quiet.

I slipped the ring back into my pocket, closing my hand over it as if to trap its warmth. It was a part of me now, just as he was. Wherever I went, however much time passed, I would always carry a piece of him.

Turning from the sea was the hardest thing I'd ever done.

The soft murmur of Coral Cove life rose to meet me as I walked up the shore. The town lay unchanged—charming, peaceful, utterly ordinary.

But *I* was not the same.

Cthulhu's world had marked me, carved itself into my soul like a scar that would never fade. Though I walked among humans, part of me would forever belong to the dark, endless depths and the god who ruled them.

And that was okay.

I didn't need to be whole.

With quiet determination, I kept moving forward.

The sand shifted beneath my feet.

The sun was setting now, streaking the sky with red and gold, painting the sea in firelight.

I glanced back once, toward the horizon. Toward him.

The pulse of the ring in my pocket throbbed faintly, a reminder. A promise.

One day, our worlds would collide again.

And when that day came, I would be ready.

CHAPTER TWELVE
EPILOGUE

The void pressed close around him, black and endless.

Cthulhu's body ached with the strain of holding the rift closed. The last of his strength bled into the battle, tentacles lashing, clawing, *defying*. The chaos creature screamed—not with sound, but with reality itself twisting and tearing under its fury.

It wanted her.

It had *always* wanted her.

And for a moment, as Maddison vanished through the closing tear, he'd almost lost himself to despair.

Almost.

He could still feel her—the soft echo of her soul thrumming against his own, faint but unbroken.

Alive.

Safe.

The pulse steadied him.

She had survived.

And that was enough.

The darkness surged again, wrapping around his limbs like a noose, but Cthulhu bared his teeth in a smile too sharp to be mortal. His roar shook the ruins that remained of his realm, a vow carried on sound and shadow.

"Across realms. Across lifetimes. Nothing will keep me from you, Maddison."

With a final violent strike, he shoved the chaos back, buying himself one ragged breath of space.

He sank beneath the waves of shadow, letting his massive form meld with the depths. His world was gone, torn apart by their battle. But the ocean—that ancient, eternal ocean—remained.

There, in the darkness beneath all worlds, he would wait.

He would heal.

And when she called for him again...he would rise.

Far above, the surface shimmered, pale and fragile as glass.

On that fragile surface, Maddison walked under a human sun, believing herself safe. Believing she had escaped.

But deep in the cracks of reality, something else was watching.

The remnants of the chaos being slithered through unseen spaces, its many eyes opening one by one. It had been beaten, yes. But not destroyed. Never destroyed.

Where Cthulhu saw Maddison as queen, the chaos saw her as a **key**.

"You cannot hide her forever," it whispered into the cold between worlds. *"She will be mine."*

The water trembled.

The tide shifted.

And somewhere, far beyond Maddison's knowing, the game began anew.

IF YOU ENJOYED *Call of Cthulhu's Heart,* you might enjoy other books in the Fae Rings series. Sign up for my newsletter and get a free book!

ALSO BY JAX WILDER

CORAL COVE SERIES

Sleighed by Love

Harvesting Love

Dawning Desire

Knead You Now

Love Rewound

Perfect Lover Spell

Haunted by Her

Red, White, and Ravished

TAROT FANTASIES SERIES

The Devil's Temptations

Strength of the Beast

Hanged Passions

Six of Cups

Death's Embrace

Queen of Pentacles

Seven of Pentacles

Ace of Wands

Three of Swords

Lovers In The Veil

<u>Two of Swords</u>

Seven of Wands

WITCHES OF CORAL COVE

From Hell With Love

COASTAL CUPID SERIES

HeartBound Souls

FAE RING SERIES

Alice and Her Mad Hatters

Bound By The Glass Slipper

STAND ALONE TITLES

Pride and Prejudice and Witches

BY LORELAI HAMILTON

Encyclopedia of Divination

Encyclopedia of Cryptids

Encyclopedia of Faeries

Tarot Tales and Magic Spells

Teenage Tarot

Arcane In Verse

The Eclectic Witch's Grimoire

Teenage Witch's Grimoire

Find Your Bliss

Tarot Reflection Journal

Tarot Refection Journal Coloring The Tarot

Dream Journal

BY MIRANDA LEVI

From A Youth A Fountain Did Flow

The Sea Withdrew

A Tear In Time

Mo(ther) Na(ture)

In Orion's Hands

BY JACKSON ANHALT

From The 911 Files

BY ISLA WATTS

A Fairy Bad Day

Surprise! You're a Vampire

Gorgeous, Gorgeous, Gorgons

Mork The Handsome Orc

Adopted By Werewolves

Bite Me If You Can

That's The Spirit!

ROSE DAWSON'S BOOK JOURNALS

My Time With The Fairies

Enchanted Escapades

Enchanted Escapades

Dewey Decimal Diaries

Siren's Songbook

Pride and Prejudice

Bibliophile's Bounty

Book of Books Journal

Pages & Passages Reading Journal

Bookworm's Companion Reading Journal & Tracker

ABOUT THE AUTHOR

Jax Wilder is a passionate romance author hailing from a charming small town nestled in the picturesque Pacific Northwest. With a heart full of love and an unyielding belief in the power of happily ever afters, Jax weaves enchanting tales of love and connection that leave readers captivated.

Jax's novels are a reflection of her commitment to celebrating the magic of love, and her characters' journeys mirror the warmth and happiness she has found in her own life. Join her on the enchanting journey of love, passion, and enduring connection through her heartfelt romance novels.